.chell, Chase,
)50-

G46   The ghost of Eden.
1995

$17.95

Chicago Public Library

REFERENCE

KER & TAYLOR

ALSO BY CHASE TWICHELL

Northern Spy (1981)
The Odds (1986)
Perdido (1991)

THE GHOST OF
EDEN

CHASE TWICHELL

Ontario Review Press ✦ Princeton

Library of Congress Cataloging-in-Publication Data

Twichell, Chase, 1950-
The Ghost of Eden : poems / Chase Twichell.
I. Title.
PS3570.W47G46 1995   811'.54—dc20   95-7912
ISBN 0-86538-083-X (hard cover)

ACKNOWLEDGMENTS

I'm indebted to the John Simon Guggenheim Memorial Foundation for a
Fellowship which gave me a whole year to work on this book. Thanks also to
the editors of the following magazines, where poems were first published,
sometimes in earlier forms: *Adirondack Life:* "The Immortal Pilots." *Antaeus:*
"Dirt," "Recorded Birds." *The Black Warrior Review:* "Corporate Geese."
The Georgia Review: "Touch-Me-Not." *The Iowa Review:* "Car Alarm," "Aisle of
Dogs," "Silver Slur." *Lips:* "Outgrown Music." *The Nation:* "Snow in
Condoland," "The Whirlpool." *The New England Review:* "The Devil I Don't
Know," "Animal Graves," "The Rule of the North Star," "Bear on Scale,"
"Stripped Car." *The New Yorker:* "City Animals." *Ontario Review:* "Girl With Sad
Face," "The Ruiner of Lives," "The Pools," "The Smell of Snow," "Sleeping
Paint." *The Paris Review:* "Bad Movie, Bad Audience," "A Seduction." *The
Southern Review:* "Ghost Birches." *Willow Springs:* "Little Snowscape," "White
Conclusion." *The Yale Review:* "The City in the Lilac." "Ghost Birches,"
"Dirt," "The Immortal Pilots," and "Snow in Condoland" were reprinted in
Poems for a Small Planet: Contemporary American Nature Poetry, University Presses of
New England, 1993. The epigraph is taken from a letter to Charles Brown
that Keats wrote in Rome on 30 November 1820, three months
before his death.

For Russell Banks, and in memory of Florence Martin Chase

I have an habitual feeling of my real life having past,
and that I am leading a posthumous existence.

—Keats

CONTENTS

I 🐾 ANIMAL GRAVES

The mower flipped it belly up,
a baby garter less than a foot long,
dull green with a single sharp

stripe of pale manila down its back,
same color as the underside
which was cut in two places,

a loop of intestine poking out.

It wouldn't live,
so I ran the blades over it again,

and cut it again but didn't kill it,

and again and then again,
a cloud of two-cycle fuel smoke
on me like a swarm of bees.

It took so long
my mind had time to spiral
back to the graveyard

I tended as a child
for the dead ones, wild and tame:
fish from the bubbling green aquarium,

squirrels from the road,
the bluejay stalked to a raucous death
by Cicero the patient, the tireless hunter,

who himself was laid to rest
one August afternoon
under a rock painted gray, his color,

with a white splash for his white splash.

Once in the woods I found the skeleton
of a deer laid out like a diagram,

long spine curved
like a necklace of crude, ochre spools
with the string rotted away,

and the dull metal shaft of the arrow
lying where it must have pierced

not the heart, not the head,
but the underbelly, the soft part
where the sex once was.

I carried home the skull
with its nubs of not-yet-horns
which the mice had overlooked,

and set it on a rock
in my kingdom of the dead.

Before I chopped the little snake
to bits of raw mosaic,

it drew itself
into an upward-straining coil,
head weaving, mouth open,

hissing at the noise that hurt it.

The stripe was made
of tiny paper diamonds,
sharp-edged but insubstantial,

like an x-ray of the spine
or the ghost beginning to pull away.

What taught the snake to make itself
seem bigger than it was,
to spend those last few seconds

dancing in the roar
and shadow of its death?

Now I see, though none exists,
its grave:

harebells withered in a jar,
a yellow spiral
painted on a green-black stone,

a ring of upright pine cones for a fence.
That's how the deer skull lay in state

until one of the neighborhood dogs
came to claim it,

and carried it off to bury
in the larger graveyard of the world.

II 🐗 GIRL WITH SAD FACE

Silence—that was her chosen music.
Not literal silence, but space
free of all human presence,

something more like blankness,
or the musical emptiness of wind.

When she scratched with a stick
on the hanging scrolls of the birches,
the waxy surface resisted.

It stayed a pure blank.
No ink could mark it.

Only the purplish splash of birdshit
in berry season, and the first rain

erased that easily. Rain is a blankness,
and the brook, which says only one thing.

It says it knows nothing of human sadness,

doesn't remember the trees
that fell across it, rotting into shadows,
or the slim shadows of the trout.

These things don't stay in its memory.
It has none. The music it makes is only

the sound of water following the laws.

When I'm unhappy I look back
into the face that was my child-face,

which knew itself to be sad
and so said nothing to humans,

a girl with the sound of leaves for a voice,

who built for herself a shelter of sticks
and white bark in the woods, and crawled in.

When I want her
I look for her among the rusty prongs
and antler-velvet of the sumac

on the far side of the brook,
listen for the words she will speak

in one of the animal languages,
which contain mostly silence.

She's the animal I can't see

but know is there,
her eyes resting on me

asking *why am I alone?*
which is also my question to her.

III 🐗 THE POOLS

I used to look into the green-brown
pools of the Ausable, the places
where the pouring cold slowed,

and see a mystery there.
I called it God for the way
it made my heart feel crushed

with love for the world outside myself,

each stone distinct and magnified,
trembling in the current's thick lens.

Now when I can't sleep
I say as a prayer
the names of all the little brooks,

Slide and Gill and Shadow,
and the names of the river pools
I fished at dusk,

working my way upstream through
slow sliding eddies and buckets of froth,

the flume, the bend, Hull's Falls, the potholes.
It's like saying the names
of the dead and the missing—

the Ausable, the Boquet, the Opalescent—

though their waters still
rush down over the gray ledges
toward Lake Champlain.

The flume was always
full of bark-colored shadows,

shafts of green light fallen
from the pines, and the silver swirls

of rising trout where now
the gray-fleshed hatchery fish
feed on the damaged magic.

Sleepless, I call to mind
the high granite walls
scored in the thaws,

the banks of black-stemmed ferns.

I lie again on a warm rock
and feel the hand of God on my back,

and feel it withdraw
in the exact instant the sun
withdraws its treasure from the water—

a tiny dissonance,
like bad news forgotten for a moment
but the shadow of its anxiety holding on,

making a little cloud of its own.

It was the thing outside the human
that I loved, and the way

I could enter it,
the muscle-ache of diving

down into the cold, green-brown spangles,

myself a part of the glimmering blur,
the falling coins of light.

Scraps of that beauty survive
in the world here and there—

sparks of rain in the pine candles,
a leaf turning in underwater currents,

then lost in the smoke of faster water.

Sometimes I glimpse the future
in the evenings. It appears
like a doe on silencing moss,

foraging among pocked leaves,
drinking the last light in the pools.

It doesn't even raise its head
to look at me. I'm not a danger to it,

trapped as I am in the purely human.

IV 🐗 LITTLE SNOWSCAPE

Consciousness ends, says the snow,
and in the meantime it's a window
left open in winter—

the cold is the same inside and out.

The great tracts of dreamland
stretch away under the vanishing balsams.

It's that point in the afternoon
when the sparks in the fresh contours

begin to go out, and shadow flakes
darken the falling air.

I'm an animal
shivering in the Godlike glitter,

the burial of earth by light
and then by light's extinction.

I want to eat, like the cold shadow,
and to be eaten, like the cold brightness.
They are my parents.

Already my tracks fill with a numb blue,

the little steps I've taken across the blur,
the white concealment,
my lies to myself.

I stand on the seam between two worlds
and think I'll never have to choose between

this one and the dead one.

My cells are made of this one,
so if it continues, I continue.
But when I look up I see that the snow

falls from a fountain that is not immortal.

V 🦊 THE RUINER OF LIVES

Who knows how things end up
spliced together in the mind.

Last night the car was lugging
up the long hill toward home
when a fox came sleepwalking

out of the alders onto the road.
Something was wrong with it.
It listed a little to one side

and moved without fox-quickness,
not sniffing, not scared,
but calm, almost formal,

with a yellow opacity in its eyes

as if it had recently
been dreaming of being blind.

It stood staring down the double barrel
of the headlights till I stopped the car.

Who knows why, but at that moment
five words came awake in my mind:

God the ruiner of lives—

a line of graffiti I once saw
sprayed on a pink wall in the tropics.
Now five sharp stars in a northern night,

shaken out of their sleep.

It was only August, but already
the uppermost leaves of the stricken maples
were ragged and red,

and the small curled leaves
of the barren apples
skittered across the road.

The fox and I—who was our ruiner?

I with the sin of despair
for the world my species has spoiled,

the fox with its hunger,
its rabies, its dirty coat
slung over a frail skeleton.

A fox of the future
digging in the underbrush
for our remains will find

more trash than bones.

I laid my hand over my heart
to put out the fire lit by this idea,
and stroked and stroked as if it were

a terrorist I could cure of its rage
with kindness and animal calm.

The yellow eyes went on dreaming
the car, the road curved into the dark.

Poor fox, poor mystic,
attracted to a light it can't explain.

A light that drives away,
and leaves us both
here under the cold,

crumbling trees of heaven.

VI 🐗 THE IMMORTAL PILOTS

The noise throws down
twin shadows, hunting shadows
on a black joy ride.

They roar up the silver vein of the river
and out over the stony peaks,

which have been shrunken to a luminous
green musculature on the screens.
Who are the pilots, too high to see

the splayed hearts of deer tracks

under the apple trees, or smell
the cider in the fallen fruit?

Who are the vandals that ransack
the wilderness of clouds?

Below them, a thin froth of waterfall
spills from a rock face.
They see its sudden wreckage,

its yielding gouts,

and the wind tear into the papery
leaves of the poplars, roughing them up

so the undersides show—
a glimpse of paleness

like a glimpse of underwear.

The pilots are young men,
and still immortal.

Already in the cold
quadrants of their hearts
they imagine the whole world

flowering beneath them. It feels
like love, like being with a woman
who flowers beneath them,

so that they wonder
how it would feel to go on
riding the young green world that way,

to a climax of spectral light.

VII SNOW IN CONDOLAND

I enter the orchard at nightfall
when it's hard to tell
the clots of late spring snow

from the apple blossoms,
the dead from the living,

though the mind has no trouble
with snow as a flower,
snow as a corsage

it can press inside its heavy book.
I could go on turning the pages
forever, so vivid

are the images there,
so perfectly preserved.
Their forms grow vaguer in the yards

as the slow light falls on swingsets,

paved culs-de-sac, mailboxes,
doghouses, acres of cold cars,
the whole stilled ocean of roofs.

The orchard has been gone
for a decade, and still the sentences
push through the laden branches,

into each frozen complex
of white on white.

It fascinates me,
the way language smudges and erases
and redraws what it wants for itself.

Even now the apples
are ripening somewhere,

inside the cold petals maybe,
in the dark, still infant part,

where a faint pink fever
was once suppressed.

VIII ❦ CAR ALARM

It must have been the combination,
the sunset plus the noise,

that was so unnerving. Sirens,
car and burglar alarms are nothing—
they go off all the time.

They're background music. This one
yowled like a mechanical Doberman
from the new Mercedes.

The owner wasn't home.
Someone had already called the cops.

That's all, yet half a dozen neighbors
stayed outside milling around in the street

because the sunset was so eerie,
the pink and orange of a spreading fire

with heavy green occlusions welling up

above the roofs, like something
burning and growing at the same time.

One minute I'm folding laundry and the next
I'm standing on the front stoop
under a sky that can't be natural,

and my heart is barking please please

please tell me what to feel
when everything I love—
that I just this instant realize I love—

blisters in the sudden radium of fear.

IX 🐗 BAD MOVIE, BAD AUDIENCE

Matinées are the best time
for bad movies—squad cars
spewing orange flame, the telephone

dead in the babysitter's hand.
Glinting with knives and missiles,

men stalk through the double
wilderness of sex and war

all through the eerie
fictions of the afternoon.
The audience is restless,

a wicked ocean roughing up its boats.

It makes a noise I seem to need.
The ruby bracelet

clinks against the handcuff,
all the cars make squealing sounds.
The kid in front of me

wants more candy,
rocks in her velvet seat. *Shut up,*

says her mother, maybe seventeen.
Just shut the fuck up.

The corpses of the future
drift across the galaxy with nothing

in their stiff, irradiated hands.

In our ears the turbo revs,
the cheekbone cracks,
a stocking slithers to the floor.

Cocteau said film is death at work.

Out of the twilight
a small voice hisses

Shut up, just shut the fuck up.

X 🐖 THE DEVIL I DON'T KNOW

It seems to be the purpose of mourning

to change the mourner, to tip over,
in the end, the urn that holds the grief.

When a loved person dies,
elegy formalizes that work.

But what if it's the holy thing itself,
the thing beseeched with prayer,
that's the deceased? What good is elegy then?

I was pushing my cart through the sharp
fluorescence of the supermarket,

lost in this question. People pawed
through the shrink-wrapped meats

which look like body parts to me
since I stopped eating them,

things that should have been buried,

and I thought, to what should I pray?
I'd always prayed to the ineffable
in its body the earth,

to the sacred violence of storms,
huge tracts of seaweeds rocked in the dark,

the icy crystals of the stars above the snow,
the mystery untamable and pure.

So what should I pray to now
in the hour of my abandonment?

Should I stand in my shining cart and shout
that the age of darkness is upon us?

Or turn inward to the old disciplines
and wander like a disembodied soul
through the wreckage, honoring my vows,

faithful to the end? A pilgrim
grown bright and clean as a flame,

eating only the gifts of the plants
and trees, what fattens among leaves

or swells in the soil underfoot.
Pure offerings. That means

no to fellow creatures bloated with steroids,

no to the heavy metals that shine
in the mackerel like tarnished silver,

no to the black-veined shrimp
in their see-through shells.

No to the embalming liquids
injected with needles,

no to the little chops packaged in rows
like a litter of stillborn puppies,

no to the chickens' sputum-colored
globules of fat, no to the devil I know.

The circular blade started up in the deli,

pink sheets of ham drooping into the plastic
glove of the man behind the counter.

What am I, an empty vessel waiting
for some new holy thing to come pour itself
into me? Where is the new divine?

I want to feed myself
into the machines of grief

and come out changed, transformed,
a new soul with a new consciousness.

I want a new inscrutable to worship,

to turn to in times of uncertainty and fear.
But there's only
the soft hiss of the lobster tank,

and the one surviving lobster, just sold,
waving its pegged claws from the scale.

A small swordfish gleams behind the glass.
Dear higher power, dear corpse of the world,

gutted, garnished, laid out on ice.

XI 🐗 THE WHIRLPOOL

Someone at the party said it was impossible
to imagine the death of the species

(the cocktails sparkling and the voices
murmuring together of life's tenacity),

but I could imagine it.

I stood looking down from the balcony
at the Hudson's starved and beaten ghost,
the high walls of the stone canyons

still catching light
though the big flame of the day was guttering.

A voice said, Sure, the dinosaurs died.
But they still roam the pristine world

and thrash their spiny tails in our imaginations,
don't they? That's a kind of life.

The city below me kept folding
in on itself in a sickening swirl,
the lines of traffic

feeding through the intersections
like the wild spirals of DNA, red and white
(their lights in the dusk just coming on).

It was like looking into the head of a peony
vivid with ants, stemless,

a skull with its innards devoured,

all shell, all aftermath,
white in places like driftwood or bone,
though I didn't say that.

I can hear the voices of the dead out here,

murmuring together of life's fragility.
Drawn by the density of human sound,

they turn around us in a slow wheel,
though we are not their center of gravity.
What a whirling paradise this is,

this suck of conscious seconds

drawing me into the day's black ending,
and far below me the city's crawling stars,

each one a second in the dream.

XII 🐗 TOUCH-ME-NOT

I have to fight in myself the desire
to put down the pen and go outside
where the tufted, seed-heavy grasses

float on the slow river of August.

When a poem touches on the act of writing,
it breaks the dream. That's why this one
opens as it does—defensive,

already split between wanting to know
where it's going and wanting not to know.

I lie down under the sketchy canopy
of the field with my face close
to the cellar smell of earth

where the white shoots gleam
doubled up in the dew
in their little preserve.

I'd rather watch the bees
work the wildflowers

than follow the cursive tracks
wherever it is they go.
Something, maybe the soul,

says language is a whip that hurts it,

slicing open the still-forming
sky-colored chicory flowers,
leaving the flayed stems to say

what the truth is.
I'd rather listen to the brook,

its words always garbled
just out of earshot.

It's not the words themselves
that scare the soul,
but their unearthly gleam,

the gleam the pallbearers follow
first to the church
and then to the hole in the ground.

One day what has always been true
will no longer be true, just like that.

If this were a poem about my own death,
I'd know how to make the rasp and honey
of the August field take on that meaning,

and I'd rest for a while in the image
of my body married to the black
beloved dirt, the microbes, the rains,

the weed seeds sending out
their slender filaments of root.

But it's not my death that's set
like a steel trap at the end of the poem.
It's the earth's, upon whose body I lie,

and toward whom the ant trails of ink all lead.

This world has always been widow and widower,
the one we leave bereft

when we slip into the place
without sunlight, without leaves.
Now what has always been true

is no longer true. I want to lie down
and swim in the shade with the trout lilies
to avoid saying it.

The earth as it has always been
is saying its goodbyes. Another world

will overrun the emptiness,

but I love this one.
I let it hold me longer than I mean to,
the feather-leaves of yarrow,

the vetches' frail tendrils,
and the spotted touch-me-nots

which give such an intimate response
if you touch one of the tiny swollen pods—
faintly striped, fat in the middle,

and containing a tense spring,
an unspiraling release

that flings the seeds in all directions.
I touch, and between my fingers

the miniature violence spends itself.

Like the seeds I'm propelled
toward some future field,

which glows from far off
like the idea of plutonium,
immortal and alien.

When I hear the wind taking leave
of the stricken trees—the beeches,
the birches, the red spruce—

or the wet-rag-on-glass sound of the phoebe

in her nest of lichens under the eaves,
when I walk in the ferns' green perfume

or lie with my face among cool roots
and sprouts all intertangled and doomed,

I'm imagining what will happen
to the soul in me,

which feeds on these things,
and which I fear will go on living

after the loved world dies.

XIII 🐗 RECORDED BIRDS

I was watching the suffering on TV,

one of the wars—
smoke and broken houses and bafflement,

a row of children lying under a tarp,
the sound of weeping.

The ruins from the last war
had not yet healed. Vines were undoing

what was left of the walls.

Small birds with split tails
twittered on the soundtrack,
swaying in the leaves

behind the reporter and his microphone,

their voices netted
from the wilderness of sound in space,

centuries of animal and human voices

preserved in the airwaves,
immortal, without destination,
perpetually travelling

through what looks from here
like an ocean. If only we knew how,

we might call back to us the sounds
of those that have departed earth,
if only we could find a way

to trap the shards, the long
ribbony trails. Keats, Jesus—

the voices I would love to hear.
Walt Whitman. Dickinson.

My ancestors, all the way back.
The first birds, before they were named.

The silence of the first fox stalking them.

XIV 🐗 DIRT

I was standing in the frozen garden
spreading wood ashes, wondering
about the space in which music plays,

how it also gets recorded,
and the dirt in a record's grooves,

the scratchy, friendly, pre-tech sound of it,

like waves almost, a frictional circular
crosscurrent, a counterpoint.

I had been reading my will,
writing my whims in the margins
in pencil, just fooling around with ideas

about the dispersal of my property,
part of which I was standing on,

asking myself who would most love
to put down one of my books

and come outside
to stand here on the frost-crusted soil,

the mountains already casting
their blue winter shapes
down into the valley.

If age is a measure
of the world's weight in us,
I'll someday fill to overflowing,

a little flood of dust,

and will then lie intimate with dirt,
or be blown in the form of ash
into the cells of the blossoming woods.

There I was,
looking down at the remnant stalks,
collapsed tomato skins,

horse manure still in its rounded
tea-colored briquets, like petrified grass,
a sort of vegetable fossil.

I don't want to die, but all knowledge
leads to the one conclusion, after all.

Suddenly the will with its silly ribbons
and wax seal seemed nothing but
an inventory of delusions

for the time when I'll become

the soil riding in the black grooves,
the compost layered with leaf-ghosts,

a crumb of what I was when I was alive.

XV 🐻 BEAR ON SCALE

Even dead,
her weight resists the rope harness—

she is not a pet, not a slave.

Although he knows the bear is female,
the man still calls her *it* or *him*.
Two hundred twenty pounds,

turning slowly in the air.
They weigh about the same.

His fingers ruffle the lustrous pelt,
true black but for the long brown muzzle,

and over the small eyes clouded with refusal,

two faint brown eyebrows.
Bears have been known to climb
utility poles for the bee-buzz in the lines,

but she won't sniff the human trees
or cut her four-claw mark
on the beeches anymore,

or gouge from the oak its stinging honeycomb.

On shelves behind the man and animal:
paint cans, car wax, caulking gun.

They're in a garage. The floor is cement.
He'll have to get down on all fours

to scrub away the dark spattering

after he cuts her down,
or maybe he'll leave it there beneath the scale

for no reason he can think of.

XVI 🐗 A SEDUCTION

I had a dream so pure of form
it slipped intact from the dark:

out of a narrow cleft in granite,
a waterfall sluiced
down through damp mosses, lichens,

ferns in a glitter of thrown drops.

(I used to fish for trout shadows
there, in childhood,

where the partridgeberry trailed
its small green disks in the spray.)

But I was inside, looking out through
a crude window, a hole
in the wall of massive stones,

and saw the lit candles
overflowing on the ledge,

the long lily petals,
gray-edged and shrunken,
dropping onto the black crepe.

It was a place of remembrance
for the dead, and I thought:

the jewels in the brook
are the lights of grief.
The beloved is already dead:

all the green frailties
and sacramental waters

before the naked species
came to feed on them,

and the virulent armies went forth
leaking excrement and fuel
to colonize the last shreds of paradise.

O beautiful window cut from the dark.

In the moment of death
can I climb through the bright rectangle
into the resurrection,

a heaven preserved within myself?

I've lost the way.
O dream, come back for me.

XVII ☙ SLEEPING PAINT

When I began to paint the pictures,
there was only one of me,

a twelve-year-old slamming
the door to her bedroom so her parents
could get on with their beloved

argument in peace.

The door was blue, color of secrecy
and the furled flag of the self,

and the brush a spastic wing
that stabbed and scrubbed.

But when I was a little older
and married the paint,

colors I forced from the stubs of tubes
the art teacher saved for me,

its disobedience became my joy

and my second self,
its staining oils under my nails,
its turpentine headache,

the white rooms I could dream in
as long as there was color to spend,

rooms I could even trash if I wanted to

with wasteful spurts and smears,
rooms in which I might find

the boy I'd lie down with naked
if he were real, the mother and father

dead of their green and crimson war.

But I was half a child and the paint
scared me, carmine breaking into black

like a bad spirit muscling me
up against the smooth pale wall,
its kiss a man's kiss, not a boy's,

slipping me the secret of my secrets.

It laughs at me now, old love,
from the light sleep of its exile,

whispering of emptiness, of pleasures
and dangers, but mostly of emptiness

and the faint tracks my words leave
as they cross it.

Wherever there are two, says the paint,
one will abandon the other.

XVIII 🐗 THE CITY IN THE LILAC

Early evening is lilac time,
when the stinging insects of memory

are drawn to the heavy, half-opened
flames. I put my face into a cluster

and breathe in the purple ether.

Some memories won't sleep,
even though there's nothing left of them

but the clipped twigs of hope,
the kid sticking her face into a flower,

feeling the hard little buds of sadness

forming under her shirt, a boy's shirt.
Nothing left but a feeling, an intimation

that the world is still spoiled in secret,
that no one sees it happen.

The perfume is inside the lilac's privacy.

It can lead you to a hideout,
a fort in the leaves,
but it can also trick you and go instead

down the stairs into the purple darkness

if you're not careful, if you're still
innocent, if you're ten years old

and the man taking your picture
against the bruise-colored velvet
shows you how the color becomes you,

shows you the secret room with the sliding
door, the tiny red night-light,

the beautiful lady rising
out of the cloudy chemicals of her bath
with nothing on, so that you can see close up

the black triangle between her legs,

its tufted fur, and her face, tense and proud.
It was Mrs. M— from down the street.

But tonight the lilac doesn't smell
like the darkroom. It smells
like the melting honey of the candles

at the child's memorial, the tomboy

still in the photographer's costume,
a man's shirt, its tails
grazing the small thighs on which

a few tiny dots of blood still cling,

like the ones left on my own thighs
by the whip-sting of raspberry vines

when I went into the rough field
to smell the lilacs, and came away with

tonight's long scratch of childhood.

Inside the flower there's a black
honeycomb of rooms,

and in one of them a woman sleeps
lightly on a child's bed, dreaming
she has forgotten to lock the door,

which is soft, like a petal, and damaged.

An insect has eaten a hole in it.
It's keeping the woman separate
from the things that are already dead,

though she could see them looking in at her
if she opened her eyes. The room is lit

only by the evening sky, a faint rectangle
of window high above the city's

click and flash, its artificial moons,

its lights signalling red—you can't go.
OK now you can go.

But go silently, go secretly.

XIX 🐗 OUTGROWN MUSIC

Either innocence is taken from you
or you give it away. Truth takes it,
being the greater beauty.

Keats gave his away,
walking home late, the night birds

singing the about-to-be-outgrown music,
his hands in the moonlight holding

the heavy green apples he stole

from someone's orchard along the way.
In the false light they looked ripe.

I think he was afraid he was creating
a separate being wholly outside

his paling self—himself as he was,
himself as he would soon be,

with the forming ghost a gaunt rope

between them. It was his tether,
his leash. Death dragged him forward

and life held him back. He poured
his best poems into the world
in that state of half-detachment,

the one soon to be dead
walking beside him, mimicking

the bird's song with his warm mouth,
turning it into a human song.

That was his only company.

Keats emptied the weight of it
out of his ghost hands into the poems.

XX 🦊 WHITE CONCLUSION

What's left of the day
leaks from an orange fissure overhead,

not the scorched hole
that scientists say is there
above the sunset, but a gash

in the carbon dreamscape of sky.

The other hole I imagine
to be white-rimmed,

crusted with chemical ice

the color of fat or cancer cells,
or the froth at the mouth of a fox.

The sunset is only
tonight's unfinished watercolor

hiding the wound.
I see the gleam of weaponry in it,

far-off traffic and trash.
It's beautiful anyway,

the lacerated wilderness,

its faintening mauve above the uncut field
where the common flowers bloom as always,
live coals of hawkweed,

the vetches purple, near-invisible,
having soaked up some of the dusk.

And the white ones,
big multiplying clusters of them—

yarrow's coarse lace
and the sharp-edged daisies
growing even out of the stones in the wall.

Their white is a white that will survive us.

XXI 🐾 CORPORATE GEESE

When the big corporations began to build
their black glass palaces among the cow fields
of Princeton, New Jersey,

the hoof-chopped turf and muddy ponds
rippled for a moment in the heat waves
pushed by the bulldozers,

and then resolved themselves
into lakes and lawns, pure green slopes

on which executives could practice
their golf strokes during the hours
reserved for the health club and lunch.

And there was water gleaming in shapes
determined by experts to be
aesthetically pleasing, or tranquillizing,

or suggestive of the corporate logo.

These rival Edens lay on the flyway
of the Canada geese. The first year,

the ragged V's stopped on their way
south, landing on the clean new mirrors
beside the fresh squares of sod,

under which huge heating ducts criss-crossed,

melting the first snow as it fell, and making
a grid of shining grass, permanently green.

The geese stayed on, and more came.
Cars stopped to watch the vast flocks

preening and paddling, flying short aimless
missions over the town, squadrons
of gray-brown bombers landing and taking off,

the faraway north in their dog-voices.

On the corporate lawns, the slimy
cylindrical droppings began to accumulate,

clogging the mowers in spring—"organic
but non-nutritive," said the town paper—

and put an end to the mid-day golfing.

Various kinds of lights and noises
had no effect, and talk of poison and humane
relocation caused a public outcry.

So on they stayed, hundreds in each paradise:

Merck Pharmaceuticals, Cosmair, FMC,
Johnson & Johnson, Proctor & Gamble,

Merrill Lynch, the Princeton Plasma Lab.

We've lost our way, said the geese
in their muted barking. Something in nature's

gone wrong, wrong. They said it
over and over, but no one heard them.

It sounded like squabbling, or mild outrage.

Teeming in their artificial south,
they gorged on breadcrumbs from the hand
of the future,

where their querulous voices
vanished in the hush of the wild grass

and the rain fell on dead cars,
the trackless contoured fields,

and, rising from a slag of black jewels,
the great steel skeletons

scrawled with the tags and logos of the dead,
picked clean by the locusts of their own creation.

XXII 🐗 STRIPPED CAR

There's something in me that likes
to imagine the things I'm afraid of,

for example, the future.
I don't mean the celestial fireworks

from melting reactors, or New York
under six feet of sea water,
but the future in its most intimate,

most probable forms—vignettes
subversive enough to slip through the radar.

That's how I come to be crouched
behind a stripped car wondering

would it be too dangerous
to piss in the street?
It would, I'm a woman.

So I go on holding it,
distracting myself by trying to remember
every fruit I've ever eaten,

their exact textures and flavors.
So far the most exotic is the custard apple.

I use up a whole hour of daylight
and then another—apricot, blueberry, plum—

calves cramping from having to stay low,
waiting behind a car pitted

with the acne of automatic fire.

There are still too many guns
walking around out there,
and no one I know,

so I'm waiting for twilight at least.
Is everyone alone now?

The wind says so. It says
a winter is coming without oil.

It bites to get my attention
and scatters a few leaflets,
pictures of a blackened car,

a city that seems to catch on fire
every sunset, though there's
little enough to burn. Stone only chars.

This isn't a likeness of the future, is it?
Every person in the street a stranger?

Will a word like 'neighbor' survive this?

I fired a gun once. It smelled rancid, sour,
like bad food. It hurt my shoulder

and left a wound of oil on my shirt.

My mind is thinking of sleep again.
Sleep lets things escape—my pocket-knife

vanished through a knife-sized hole.

There's nothing to cut,
no guava, nectarine, winter pear,

and nothing left of the car at all,
not even the rear-view mirror
I was counting on,

hoping my face could tell me
it was safe to go home, and where is that?

A place with a bed
and a desk where I sit and plot
next year's garden on graph paper.

The skin of a tangelo is faintly pebbly,
easy to peel, but the sweetest citrus

is the satsuma, then the clementine.
If I had to choose between natural
disaster and a firing squad,

I'd take the river of lava any day.

Hurricane, tidal wave, tornado, drought.
I want the earth, which is waiting
under the sidewalk, to be the one.

Not any of these human shadows
sporting their silhouetted guns.
There were gun shadows before,

but the two worlds overlapped,
guns and the amber waves of grain.

It's hard to say whether bramble fruits
actually have skins. Does a raspberry?
Does each tiny globe have its own?

How will I live without the earth?

In a stripped car, unable to piss
when I want to, all the time cold?

Maybe weapons interbred with humans,
and a strain of hybrids was born,
half metal, half flesh.

I know there's an enemy—
look at all the damage it's doing.
Maybe it's still a baby,

its weak neck wobbling as its carriage
lurches over the broken pavement.

But probably by now
it's a sulking adolescent
starting to look like serious trouble,

with a silky little shadow-moustache
and a gun. Who'll kill it? Will I?

What if it doesn't look like an enemy?
What if it comes disguised as a savior,
or resembles nothing so much as hunger,

so that everyone has his own
private piece to kill? Will we do it?

XXIII 🐾 THE RULE OF THE NORTH STAR

I should be ashamed to love
the first hard frost the way I do,

the way it glitters
over the surface of everything,

erasing whatever's human.

But I'm not. So I stand for a minute
in the crystalline grass
with an armload of frozen firewood,

letting a little of the ruthlessness
enter my bones, breathing
white sparrows into the air.

Oh, I know where the logic leads.
If the lights of the town

spoil the dark... If the trucks
downshifting on the Cascade hill
infect the wind...

If humanity's the enemy, the enemy is me.

But there's something in me, an arrow
that points toward wilderness,

toward the mountain that governs
such loves, its ledges high enough
to have caught last night's

faint halo of snow.
Wherever I am, in all weathers,
I look up, and it's there,

it always has been, rising even
above the charred towers of cities,
under the north star which glints down

onto its sharp summit,
and onto each withered grass blade,

each rattling pod, each burned-out car,
each smaller star of broken glass.

The mountain which has no name
burns in the distance

with a beautiful, radical plainness,

ledges bright with snowmelt.
It's the shrine,

the afterimage of the moment in which
I first imagined the world's death,

and knew at the same stroke
that though it would survive in some form,

it would not survive in this form.

The firewood aches in my arms.
Its smoke will cross over,

touching both the ash in the fireplace
and the face of the mirage.

The north star
comes out earlier each evening.

It shines down onto the cloudy
or snowy or clear-skied world,

the wars, the droughts, the famines,

the ethnic cleansings,
just as it shone on the plagues,

the witch trials, the forced marches,
the purges, the great extinctions.

It will still be the sharpest spark
in the heavens long after my death,

your death, the next death of language—

a spark that will preside over the world
we leave behind, where acres of bones

catch the starlight, and a gray wind
scribbles in the drifts of ash.

XXIV 🐕 AISLE OF DOGS

In the first cage
a hunk of raw flesh.
No, it was alive, but skinned.

Or its back was skinned.
The knobs of the spine

poked through the bluish meat.

It was a pit bull, held by the shelter
for evidence until the case
could come to trial,

then they'd put him down. The dog,
not the human whose cruelty

lived on in the brindled body,
unmoving except for the enemy eyes.

Not for adoption, said the sign.

All the other cages held adoptable pets,
the manic yappers, sad matted mongrels,
the dumb slobbering abandoned ones,

the sick, the shaved, the scratching,
the wounded and terrified, the lost,

one to a cage, their water dishes
overturned, their shit tracked around,

on both sides of a long echoey
concrete aisle—clank of chain mesh gates,
the attendant hosing down the gutters

with his headphones on, half-dancing
to the song in his head.

I'd come for kittens. There were none.
So I stood in front of the pit bull's
quivering carcass, its longdrawn death,

its untouched food, its incurable hatred
of my species, until the man with the hose
touched my arm and steered me away,

shaking his head in a way that said
Don't look. Leave him alone.
I don't know why, either.

XXV 🐇 THE SMELL OF SNOW

There's a dream I keep dreaming,

in which Russell and I
are walking with flashlights
through a stand of young birches.

There must be a low moon—
it's not quite dark.

Even without our lights we can see
animals moving through the woods,

and each appears in slightly
heightened color, as if its spirit
were manifest—

the fox nearly magenta,

the sleek bear anthracite,
deer the color of banked fire.

But when an animal moves
into one of the long, weak beams,
it turns colorless,

pale and indistinct, like falling snow.

Only in the dark does the spectral magic
survive: pack of bronze coyotes,

the raccoon's burnt-umber rings.

So we turn off the flashlights
and wander among the animals,

and neither we nor they are afraid.

That grove of birches
exists in the actual world.

It's up on the ridge above the house,
an hour and a half's climb.
Russell and I hike up there often

to stand in the stripped white trees
in winter, or to lie in summer
in the frail plumage beneath them.

We were rash to be up there
with deer season just opened,

cardboard skeletons still up in the town,
wreckage of pumpkins on the roads.

My shirt chilled me,
damp from the long climb,
and I remember thinking

it must be cold
up in the blue river where the hawk
banks on currents I can't see...

Then a door opened in the woods
and he came out, the color of charred bark.

At first I thought it was a dog,
a wild dog, then an instant later

a bear, but it wasn't a bear.
Whatever it was, I'd never seen one—

long, low-slung, heavy-muscled body,
muzzle a dark wedge, big delicate
rounded ears, brush tail like a fox,

thick curved claws in the dead leaves.

He took a few steps toward us,
his coarse coat rippling,

and I felt myself slide
into the slow-motion
story of an accident, thinking

is this my death? surprised at the way
detachment and fear were of equal size.

It was a fisher,
what the local people call a fishercat,
though it's not a cat and doesn't fish.

It's a cousin of the marten,
a tree-climber that feeds on porcupines,
snowshoe rabbits, mice and squirrels,

not yet extinct but almost never seen.

And then I smelled him.
He smelled like snow.

Not the faint industrial
sea-tang that haunts
storms blown in from the east,

but the scent of the strange
light that billows down from the vast

and citiless woodlands of the north.

When I was a child I thought
that was the smell of God because
it obscured what was human,

taking everything into its cold cremation—

the long road-scars,
house lights coming on,

pickups filling in the yards.
I looked into the small black

God-eyes of the fishercat

and saw they were empty of
any language I could extract.

In the ten seconds or so before he slipped
back into the world inside the world,
I felt my body long toward his,

a sudden carnal ache

that seduced me away from the thought
of my ashes sifted
together with my husband's,

gritty sleet blown into the leaves

and grasses, into the earth on which
the fishercat sleeps, ruts, feeds,
though that image comforts me.

But at that moment I wanted instead
to be the single

creature of his desire,

the one he would tear open,
drag off in pieces to devour,

and thus disappear
in violence into the world of his flesh,

go where his flesh goes,
even into the coyotes' hunger

when they finally pull him down,
into their scat

with its clots of hair and berry seed,

living on a while longer
in blood, piss, fur, musk,

before my bleached dust is abandoned

to the roots and leaves, and I become
the words the wind says
to the birch tatters, the song

the hawk's shadow sings to the ground,

an animal of ash dispersing
like snow in moonlight,

its spirit free of any human
vision of the afterlife,

here and then not here, like the
innocent flame of the red squirrel

crushed out in the innocent jaws.

XXVI 🐾 GHOST BIRCHES

The road crew worked all afternoon
cutting the dead birches.

Run-off from the road salt killed them,

trapped as they were on the narrow strip
left between the asphalt and the lake,

and rain-weakened. The acid
starts the yellow inflammation early,

the leaves in June already
arthritic in the cells.

We used to call them snow ghosts:

one white hidden in another.
Now they're stacked in six-foot sections,
their branches trimmed away,

and in the lake
the new emptiness heals over.

Then comes the plow of winter
straight down the valley,

pushing its wedge-shaped shadow.
All the lesser shadows move aside
as if still talking to one another,

flexible in wind, assessing their losses,
the future already upon them,

its sky-blue speckled crystals burning
down through the packed snow into the earth.

Maybe a man on the crew
with a truck of his own

will come on Saturday
to haul the white logs away, cut and split
and stack them, and he'll find them

crumbled to embers in his stove
when he comes home late and cold
from plowing after a heavy snow,

their shadows having already slipped
up the chimney to join all the other

shades of the world, the young ones
gone back to lie beside their stumps,

the old ones free to travel anywhere.

XXVII 🐗 SILVER SLUR

Nothing stays attached to what I saw,

what I glimpsed from a train.
It has no magnet for meaning.

Four men sat on a wall shooting up,

companionable. One waved at me.
Waved the needle. Ten feet away,

a man was fucking a woman from behind,
controlling her with her heavy necklace,

a bicycle chain. The budding sapling
shook as she clung to it,

her orange dress hitched up in back.
People there throw garbage out the windows.

Who cares? Four arms, four rolled-up sleeves.

The silver slur of light along the tracks.
Four arms, four rolled-up sleeves.

The orange dress hitched up in back.

XXVIII 🐖 CITY ANIMALS

Just before the tunnel, the train
lurches through a landscape
snatched from a dream. Flame blurts

from high up on the skeletal refinery,
all pipes and tanks. Then a tail of smoke.

The winter twilight looks like fire, too,

smeared above the bleached grasses
of the marsh, and in the shards of water

where an egret the color of newspaper
holds perfectly still, like a small angel

come to study what's wrong with the world.

In the blond reeds, a cat picks her way
from tire to oil drum,

hunting in the petrochemical stink.

Row of nipples, row of sharp ribs.
No fish in the iridescence.
Maybe a sick pigeon, or a mouse.

Across the Hudson,
Manhattan's black geometry begins to spark

as the smut of evening rises in the streets.

Somewhere in it,
a woman in fur with a plastic bag in her hand
follows a dachshund in a purple sweater,

letting him sniff a small square of dirt
studded with cigarette butts.
And in the park a scarred Doberman

drags on his choke chain toward another fight,

but his master yanks him back.
It's like the Buddhist vision of the beasts
in their temporary afterlife, each creature

locked in its own cell of misery,
the horse pulling always uphill
with its terrible load, the whip

flicking bits of skin from its back,
the cornered bear woofing with fear,

the fox's mouth red from the leg in the trap.

Animal islands, without comfort between them.
Which shall inherit the earth?

Not the interlocking kittens frozen in the trash.

Not the dog yapping itself to death
on the twentieth floor. And not the egret,
fishing in the feculent marsh

for the condom and the drowned gun.

No, the earth belongs to the spirits
that haunt the air above the sewer grates,

the dark plumes trailing the highway's
diesel moan, the multitudes
pouring from the smokestacks of the citadel

into the gaseous ocean overhead.

Where will the angel rest itself?
What map will guide it home?